D0422916

DECODED

<Written by>: Thomas Kingsley Troupe
<Illustrated by>: Scott Burroughs

www.12StoryLibrary.com

Copyright © 2016 by Peterson Publishing Company, North Mankato, MN 56003. All rights reserved. No part of this book may be reproduced or utilized in any form or by any means without written permission from the publisher.

12-Story Library is an imprint of Peterson Publishing Company and Press Room Editions.

Produced for 12-Story Library by Red Line Editorial

Illustrations by Scott Burroughs
Technology adviser: Greg Case

ISBN
978-1-63235-227-9 (hardcover)
978-1-63235-252-1 (paperback)
978-1-62143-277-7 (hosted ebook)

Library of Congress Control Number: 2015934331

Printed in the United States of America
Mankato, MN
October, 2015

3 2872 50146 4212

TABLE OF CONTENTS

1

OFF TO A BAD START

It wasn't like Grady Hopkins loved school, but he definitely didn't like being late for it. But that's exactly what happened Tuesday morning. The sun peeking through the venetian blinds in his room warmed up his eyelids, making them snap open.

Grady rolled over and looked at his dresser. The face of his alarm clock was dark.

Is the power out? Grady wondered sleepily.

"Grady!" his mom shouted from the basement. "What are you doing? Are you still in bed?"

He shot out of bed as if he'd been electrocuted. Stumbling around the piles of clothes on the floor, he found a pair of jeans that didn't smell too bad, a shirt he hadn't worn since last week, and some socks without holes in them.

Grady skidded into the bathroom. His light brown hair was sticking up in the back. Brushing his teeth with one hand, he slapped on as much water as he could to plaster his hair back down.

"Grady!"

"Muh mumming mah," Grady groaned through a mouthful of toothpaste. He glanced out the bathroom window and saw how high the sun was in the sky. It was late, and he was going to be even later for school.

Back in his bedroom, he snatched up his backpack and scanned his cluttered desk for his homework. He had a bad habit of leaving his work right there when he was done, but it was nowhere to be found. Opening up his pack, he saw that his folders were already tucked in, all nice and neat.

I don't remember doing that, Grady thought, but he shrugged. There wasn't time to think about anything but getting to first period . . . and fast.

As he came downstairs, Grady saw his mom waiting at the bottom of the steps. She didn't look happy.

"Was there a power outage or something?" Grady asked. He found his shoes at the bottom of the steps and tried to tug one on. For some reason his foot didn't fit.

"No, there wasn't," his mom replied. "But you're going to be late. Becky has already left."

"I think my alarm clock died or something," Grady muttered. He reached into his left shoe and found a wadded-up sock inside, jammed into the toe. When he went barefoot sometimes, he would take off his shoes and put his socks in there so he wouldn't lose them. But he couldn't recall doing that recently.

He tossed the sock aside and put on his shoes.

"All right," Grady said, standing up. "I have to blast out of here."

He grabbed his MP3 player and plugged in his earbuds. Before he hit play, he looked around the entryway, feeling as if he'd forgotten something. Over his mom's shoulder, Grady looked into the kitchen. There, on the counter, was his brown lunch bag.

"Oh, man," Grady gasped, darting into the kitchen quickly. He snatched up his lunch and tossed it into his backpack. Glancing at the microwave's digital clock, he realized it was 9:06 a.m.

Late!

Grady looked around, still amazed that he'd slept so long. It kind of bugged him that his younger sister, Becky, hadn't bothered to wait for him or even wake him up.

"What time did Becky leave?" Grady asked, zipping his backpack closed.

"She left earlier than usual," his mom said. "Said she didn't want to be late. Besides, it's not her fault you couldn't get out of bed."

"Okay, okay," Grady said, slinging his pack on. It felt heavier than usual, but he wondered if it was just because he was still half asleep.

"You need to get moving."

"Right," Grady said and headed for the door. "See you, Mom."

As he passed by, she stopped him.

"But it's never too late to hug your mom," she said with a smile.

"Yeah, okay," Grady said and couldn't resist smiling back. He gave his mom a quick hug and launched himself out the door.

Grady raced down the street, thankful that Wheatley Middle and Elementary School was only a few blocks away. He fumbled in his pocket for his MP3 player and found the play button. A couple of good songs would get him pumped and ready to race to the school's front doors.

Immediately, he could hear a twangy guitar fill his ears. A second later, some cowboy-sounding guy with an accent started singing about his tractor and his dog.

Country music?

As Grady crossed the street, he pushed the double arrow button, advancing to the next song. More twang! A couple of cowboys singing about America.

"What is going on?" Grady groaned, skipping to the next song and the next. Every single track was a country song. None of them were songs he had on his playlist at all.

He stopped, pulled his player from his pocket, and looked at the display. The Lasso Ladies. Hobie McGurt. The Ranch Hand Three. All country artists.

He double-checked to see if he'd grabbed the wrong MP3 player, but it was definitely his.

Even if it wasn't, he knew that no one in his family liked listening to that kind of music.

"Seriously," Grady mumbled, turning off the music. In his opinion, it was better to hear traffic and birds chirping than some ten-gallon-hat-wearing guy complain about his girl leaving him.

As he was about to tuck the player into his pocket, he noticed a small, white sticker on the back of the device. On it were three strange words:

LIARS OF LOP

"What the heck?" Grady exclaimed. The sticker looked as if it had been printed on a laser printer and was small enough to fit on the back of the player.

As he headed to school, later than ever, Grady wondered how so many weird things could happen to him in one morning.

DUSTED!

After checking in at the front office and getting himself a nice green tardy slip, Grady headed to his locker to drop off his bag and grab his stuff for first-period social studies. He spun the dial on his lock and pulled the metal handle to release the latch. As the door swung open, something sifted out of the bottom and onto the floor.

Sawdust?

There was enough sawdust jammed in there that it buried the bottom of his locker, and plenty of it dumped onto his shoes.

Some of the textbooks he hadn't needed for homework the night before were all but smothered in the wooden shavings.

"Okay, this is getting stupid now," Grady muttered. He groaned as he set his backpack down and brushed off his shoes. He suspected he'd need to let Marv Denny, the school custodian, know what had happened.

As he bent over, he noticed something out of the corner of his eye. There, like a bright flag in the middle of the pile, was a piece of paper.

Grady looked up and down the empty hallway before he snatched it up. He wondered if there were hidden cameras on him, watching all of the dumb stuff happening to him. Satisfied that he was alone, he looked at the paper.

LIARS OF LOP

"What is Lop?" Grady asked aloud, almost as if expecting an answer. He turned the paper over and saw there was nothing on the other side. Like the sticker on his MP3 player, it looked as if it had been printed on a laser printer.

Grady put the paper on the top shelf of his locker and pulled his social studies book from the mess. Sawdust sifted down, coating his jeans and shirt. He hung his backpack on the hook inside and headed down to the custodian's office.

"Mr. Denny?" Grady asked, peeking his head into the cluttered office. It smelled like industrial cleaner. "Are you in here?"

The space Wheatley Middle School had given its head custodian was more like a double-wide broom closet. There were mops, brooms, and shelves of cleaning solution all jammed into the space. At the far end of the room was a small desk that looked like something a teacher from 1973 might have used.

"I'm under here," a voice said from under the metal desk. "Tying my shoes."

A moment later, Marv Denny stood up. He was a short, somewhat pudgy guy in his mid-fifties, sporting some of the biggest sideburns Grady had ever seen. He had big, round glasses, the kind that changed shades depending on how light it was outside. In his dark blue jumpsuit, he looked like a race car mechanic.

"Hi," Grady said, feeling bad for bothering the guy, especially because it meant he had a mess for him to clean up. "Someone put a bunch of sawdust in my locker."

"Interesting," Marv said, sitting down. For a moment, Grady thought about the police shows that his mom sometimes watched, where the officers had to report in to the chief. The only problem was, Grady didn't feel much like a detective. "You didn't put it in there?"

"Nope," Grady said. "I wouldn't do something like that to my locker, so—"

"Oh," Marv said, scratching his left sideburn two times. "So you'd do something like that to someone else's locker?"

"No, no," Grady said. "I wouldn't. Honest. I just came to school a little late and found it like that."

"Did you give someone your locker combination?" Marv asked.

"Never," Grady said. "I wouldn't want someone to steal my junk."

Marv didn't say anything and instead seemed to study Grady for a moment.

"Or, you know, my textbooks," Grady added.

Marv stood up and went to his impressive rack of cleaning tools. From there, he extracted a small broom and a dustpan.

"Well, I'll give these to you," Marv said. "Bring them back when you're done."

Seriously? Grady thought. *Isn't that your job?*

As if he could read Grady's mind, Marv spoke.

"It isn't my job to clean up the goofy pranks you kids pull on each other," he said, handing the tools to Grady. "Especially today."

Today? What, you don't clean up on Tuesdays? Grady thought, but he took the broom and dustpan anyway.

"Okay," Grady said. "Thanks, I guess."

"Sounds like someone is messing with you, kid," Marv said. "See if you can figure out who."

As Grady left Marv's office, he looked down at his legs. There was still a bunch of sawdust flakes on his jeans.

"Sawdust . . ." Grady said, and then an obvious realization hit him. "Sawdust!"

A moment later, Grady burst through the door of the wood shop.

"Okay," Grady said, still holding the dustpan and broom. "Come clean! Who put all the sawdust in my locker?"

A dozen eighth-grade faces looked back at him. None of them looked too happy to see Grady. Mr. Houle, the industrial arts and woodworking teacher, turned from the band saw he was using.

"Excuse me?" he asked. A plume of sawdust rose up around him. "Can we help you with something?"

Grady felt the certainty of his accusation begin to slip away. Rich Murphy, who always looked like he was ready to punch someone, gave him the stink eye. Steve Zimmer smirked, as if wondering who the sixth-grade twerp was who had interrupted their class.

"Yeah," Grady said, a little more quietly. "Someone put a bunch of sawdust in my locker, so—"

"So you assumed someone from my class did it?" Mr. Houle asked. "You think someone from in here got your locker combination and filled it? Is that right?"

"Maybe?"

Mr. Houle looked around his classroom. Grady felt his heart speed-bagging inside his ribs. If he didn't do something, he was going to have more than sawdust to worry about.

"Did anyone in here—" the teacher began.

"You know, what?" Grady interrupted. "My mistake. I'm sorry I bothered you."

And before anyone could say another word, Grady left.

3

HEARTS AND KITTENS

By the time Grady cleaned up his locker and returned the cleaning supplies to Marv's office, he had only ten minutes left in his social studies class. Ms. Rollins was not pleased with him. He turned in his tardy slip and had to explain in front of the class why he had taken an extra twenty minutes to get into the classroom. He even pointed to the front of his shirt, where there was still some sawdust left as proof.

"That's enough, Mr. Hopkins," Ms. Rollins said. "Please sit down."

He took his seat next to Miles Patrick, a friend of his from the coding club. They'd nicknamed themselves and the rest of the group the Codeheads, because Grady thought "coding club" sounded too nerdy. Grady had joined only because his mom gave him an ultimatum. Either take after-school piano lessons like his sister, Becky, or spend time in the coding club. Sitting behind the keys of a computer sounded like the better option to Grady. Besides, he didn't want to have to perform at some ridiculous piano recital.

"Having a tough day?" Miles whispered.

"Dude," Grady whispered back, "you have no idea. Someone is messing with me, big time."

"Makes sense," Miles replied, before looking up to see Ms. Rollins eyeballing the two of them. Both of them kept quiet.

Why does someone messing with me make sense? Grady wondered, trying to figure out which page of his dusty textbook everyone else was following along on.

After social studies, everything else went okay until Grady hit third-period algebra. When Mr. Rashid asked for their homework, Grady pulled his worksheets from his folder. All over the sheets were little pictures of hearts, and there were flowers in the margins. There was even a little cat with giant eyes, holding a sign. The writing on the sign was carefully printed out in bold, block letters.

LIARS OF LOP

"How is this even possible?" Grady wondered aloud, looking around.

Someone has my locker combination, Grady decided. *Someone is sneaking into my locker and messing with my stuff!*

Knowing there was nothing he could do, Grady turned in his paper. To his horror, Mr. Rashid shuffled through the stack.

"Well now," Mr. Rashid mused, looking at one of the sheets. "It looks like Grady thinks this is art class."

Grady felt the back of his neck heat up a thousand extra degrees.

"Next time, Grady, can you just do the homework and leave the cutesy pictures off the sheet?"

Mr. Rashid held up Grady's worksheet for the class to see. There was a murmur in the class and a couple people laughed, including Ava Rhodes, who was also in the Codeheads.

"Cute, Hopkins," Ava said, nodding. "I didn't know you were so talented."

"Whatever," Grady said. He didn't bother explaining, knowing it would sound ridiculous. "So I like hearts and kitties. Forgive me."

"Hey, Grady," Kevin Chau whispered. "What's your favorite flower?"

"I don't know," Grady said, not letting his face change. "Maybe the Why Don't You Shut Up orchid? It's a rare, annoying flower that grows only in Mr. Rashid's algebra class."

Kevin smirked and shook his head.

Boom, Grady thought, and then a nagging thought crept in. *Wait . . . was Kevin a suspect?*

For the rest of the class, Grady couldn't concentrate. He wondered who might be messing with his locker at that very moment, planning their next stupid prank.

Liars of lop, he wondered. *Was Lop a place? If so, what was it about this Lop place that spawned liars? Was it some sort of secret prankster club?*

After algebra, Grady made his way downstairs to the second floor, where the sixth-grade lockers were. He spotted Marco Martinez, another member of the Codeheads, coming toward him in his wheelchair.

"Hello, Grady," Marco said with a quick wave. "How's it going?"

"Want the truth?" Grady asked. "Awful."

"Really?" Marco replied. "What's up?"

Grady explained all of the dumb things that had happened so far. Grady finished by showing him the paper he'd found in the sea of locker sawdust.

"Liars of Lop," Marco murmured, studying the paper. "Interesting."

4

LOCKER
SHOCKER

**At Marco's request, Grady let him keep the
LIARS OF LOP paper.**

"Keep it," Grady said. "It doesn't make any
sense to me."

"It doesn't make sense to me, either,"
Marco replied. "But I want to try a few things
with it."

"Sure," Grady replied, closing his locker.
He needed to head to gym class. "Just
remember, not everything can be solved with
a computer."

"Don't be so sure," Marco said, heading to his own class.

"Oh, this is just perfect," Grady thought when he got to his gym locker. There, all over the outside of his gym locker, were little magnets from the *Cutesy Horsey* cartoon show. Among the atrocities, there was a little purple horse with stars on its butt, an orange horse with shiny yellow hair, and a green horse with long, ridiculous eyelashes. And there was also a white, rectangular magnet with the printed words Grady was beginning to dread:

LIARS OF LOP

Okay, Grady thought, trying to pick off the magnets before anyone could notice. *So the culprit is a boy. No girl would be caught dead in the boys' locker room.*

"Whoa, nice horseys!" a voice from behind Grady cried. "I didn't know you watched that show, Grady!"

Grady turned to see his classmate Peter Yeboah standing there.

"Yeah," Grady said, unable to come up with any sort of comeback. "It's my favorite. I hear it's your favorite, too."

"My little sister watches it," Peter said, gravely. "It's terrible. Why do you—?"

"I didn't put these on here! Okay?" Grady snapped, pulling the last one off of his locker. He tucked the magnetic LIARS OF LOP sign into his pocket and tossed the horses into the trash. "Someone is messing with me."

"Well," Peter said, locking his locker up, "today's the day, I guess."

It was then that it finally hit Grady.

"April Fools'," Grady said, sitting down at the lunch table next to Marco. They usually didn't hang out with each other much outside of the coding club, but he needed his extra-smart coding colleague to know he'd figured it out.

"Yes," Marco said. "All day."

"That's why people are playing pranks on me, I meant," Grady said. "It's stupid April 1st today. Wow."

They both looked up to see Ava heading their way. She sat down on Marco's other side.

"What are you guys up to?" she asked. "The Codeheads don't usually meet until *after* school."

It suddenly seemed strange to Grady that they were all sitting together during lunch, especially when they usually sat with their other friends.

"I cracked the code," Marco said.

"Wait," Ava said. "What code?"

"Yeah," Grady said, confused once more. "What code are you talking about?"

"Liars of lop," Marco said, pulling his laptop from the backpack slung over the back of his wheelchair. "It's an anagram."

"You mean like a telegram?" Grady asked.

"What, are we living in the Wild West?" Ava asked. "Who even knows what telegrams are anymore?"

"An anagram," Marco corrected patiently. "It's a word or phrase made up by rearranging the letters to spell something else. For example, the word 'tea' could be an anagram of 'eat.' I wrote a program that took the phrase 'liars of lop' and calculated all the different ways the letters could be rearranged."

He opened his laptop and showed them a program he had up on the screen. The program displayed a number of phrases. Grady leaned forward to read some of them.

"'Fall is poor,' 'All roof sip,'" he said. "This is all a bunch of nonsense."

"Right," Marco said. "But of the 800-something nonsense phrases I found, one of them made sense."

"Which one?" Grady asked.

"What you said earlier," Marco replied. "April Fools'."

"Huh?" Grady said, feeling a bit disappointed. "I was hoping you had a name so I knew who to exact my revenge upon."

Ava laughed.

Grady turned his lunch bag upside down. What followed was a loud clank and a groan.

There, on the table, was Grady's "lunch." A bag of cauliflower, a bunch of broken saltine crackers, and an unopened can of beets. And no can opener.

"Of course!" Grady cried. "They got to my lunch, too."

He shook the bag in anger and something else dropped out. It was a piece of paper, folded into fourths.

Ava picked up the mysterious note.

"You sure you don't want the beets?" Grady asked. "I'm sure this cauliflower is delicious, too."

"Nope, I'm good," Ava replied as she shook her head and unfolded the paper. She studied it carefully.

"Let me guess," Grady muttered. "Liars of lop?"

"No," Ava said, turning the paper around for the two of them to see. "Not even close."

5

NOBODY'S FOOL

Grady looked at the words listed on the page over and over again.

"Payback of the rigorous ballyhoo," he read aloud. He turned and saw that Marco was doing the same. "What's the deal?"

Marco made some sort of clicking noise with his mouth. From all the months that Grady had known the guy, he knew it meant Marco was thinking. Ava watched the two of them and smiled wide and crooked.

"This person is seriously messing with you," she said.

"Yeah, I kind of got that," Grady snapped, looking again at the "lunch" that had been swapped out of his locker. Not only did the prankster want him to look stupid, but they wanted him to starve, too!

"Well, it's pretty clear what this is," Marco said.

"Yeah," Grady sighed. "One of those anagram things again, right?"

Marco nodded.

"So, let's just run it through your anagram program and see what it kicks out at us," Grady said. "We can read what kind of dumb message this April Fools' clown has for me."

Ava handed the note to Marco, who took it and studied it some more.

"The only problem," she said, nodding toward the page, "is that with every extra letter that's added to the message, the different combinations of word possibilities multiplies."

Grady nodded. "So it'll be harder to figure out the message," he said. "Well, that's just great."

Marco typed something into his laptop, and Grady watched. In a matter of seconds, he had the words entered. His finger hovered over the ENTER button.

"What's the matter?" Grady asked. "Aren't you going to see what we get?"

Marco nodded. "I'm just checking to make sure I didn't spell anything wrong," he said, running his fingers along the words. "If I mistype one thing, the string of results we get will be very different and could lead us down the wrong path."

Grady sighed and looked around the lunchroom. His usual gang of jock friends were giving him strange looks, as if wondering why he was sitting with Marco and Ava. He smirked at their table but studied them closely.

Is one of those guys behind this? Grady wondered. He watched the way Ajay Dhawan ate his chips and laughed at something Brett Robbins said. *Are they laughing at all the dumb stuff that happened to me today? Did they do it?*

"I heard you were late for school today," said a voice to Grady's right. Standing with her lunch tray in her hands was his younger sister, Becky. Her best friend, Sofia Cardenas, stood next to her.

"Yeah," Grady said, keeping his eye on anyone else in the lunchroom who seemed to be watching him for too long. "My alarm clock died."

"Everyone heard about the flowery homework, too," Becky said, laughing. "What is going on with you?"

Grady turned to her. He knew his sister was a bit of a gossip, but now he was getting upset.

"Seriously? People are talking about that?" Grady asked. "Even in fourth grade? What, is this a slow news day here, or what?"

"Calm down, bro. It's a small school. When dumb stuff happens, word gets around," Becky laughed and nodded at the table. "Nice lunch."

"Okay," Grady said, waving her off. "Go on, get out of here. We've got stuff to do."

"Whatever," Becky said, and in a matter of seconds, she and Sofia disappeared into the crowd.

Marco raised his eyebrows, and Ava ate her sandwich. It looked like something with peanut butter and Marshmallow Fluff. Grady glared at the can of beets.

"So, what'd you find?" Grady asked. "Anything?"

Marco turned his laptop toward Grady. "All kinds of things."

Grady looked at the gigantic list of phrases. There were thousands and thousands of them. He cringed as Marco dragged his scroll bar down to reveal even more. They all seemed like nonsense. Nothing gave him any sort of answer or clue as to who was pranking him, or why.

"This is so hopeless," Grady said. He noticed that the very first word was the same as Marco scrolled down, and this made up more than 80,000 of the entries.

"They definitely didn't make it easy," Marco agreed, sitting back in his wheelchair. "And I put in code for the program to display only dictionary words. If I took that restriction out, we'd end up with close to 600 sextillion possibilities."

"So, a lot, basically," Grady grumbled.

"Do you know anyone who'd want to mess with you?" Ava asked. "Do you have any enemies or anything?"

Grady shrugged and looked around. He couldn't think of anyone who would go to all of the trouble to make his day miserable. Sure, he joked around and played some pranks of his own, but they weren't elaborate and didn't make anyone look ridiculous.

"Not really," he said. "But then again, it's April Fools' Day, one of the dumbest days ever."

"Weird," Ava said. "I figured someone like you would like April Fools' Day."

"Not even a little bit," Grady said. "If you're going to mess with someone, you do it on a day when no one is expecting it. Not when everyone has their guard up."

The bell rang, signaling the end of lunch. They all gathered up their things, and Grady threw everything but the can of beets away. Though they were easily his least favorite food, he didn't think it was cool to throw them out.

Then, something occurred to Grady.

"Hey," he said to Marco and Ava. "Are you guys going outside for recess?"

Marco looked to Ava and both of them shrugged.

"I don't have to go," Ava said.

"Neither do I," Marco added.

"Maybe we can mess with that anagram thing a little more," Grady said. "I might have an idea."

ANAGRAM EXAM

Grady, Ava, and Marco went into the computer room after lunch, opting to spend their twenty minutes of recess trying to crack the code. Mrs. Donovan, the computer science teacher and their coding club adviser, was in there, eating her own lunch.

"Hey, Mrs. D," Grady said. "Can we try something really quick?"

Mrs. Donovan nodded, still chewing part of her sandwich. After she swallowed, she spoke up. "Of course."

"We're going to work on decrypting an anagram," Marco said, wheeling over to his usual workstation in the room.

"Sounds like fun," Mrs. Donovan replied before diving back into her lunch.

"So what's your idea," Marco asked, opening his laptop again.

"Well, whoever is messing with me probably wants to take some credit for the pranks they've been pulling, right?" Grady said. "I mean, I know I'd want my victim to know it was me who pranked them."

"Maybe," Ava said, but Grady noticed she was also tinkering with some sort of device she and Marco had been working on. "Sorry! I'm obsessed with getting this thing to work. Let me know if you guys need me."

"Will do," Marco replied and studied the giant list of results they'd pulled up from the latest anagram. "I'm still not sure how that helps. How does this narrow our search, Grady?"

"Look at the list," Grady said. "There are no names in there."

Marco scrolled through the seemingly endless list of phrases, his eyes darting back and forth across the screen. After a few moments, he nodded his head.

"You're right," he said.

"So maybe your program doesn't consider names as words," Grady said. "You know?"

Marco nodded. He pulled up a website for anagrams and scrolled through the page.

"What are you doing?" Grady asked.

"When I devised my home-cooked anagram decoder, I borrowed a few things from this website," Marco said. "It had a good foundation for me to build the program, but it was also very dependent on the server."

Grady watched as Marco clicked a few keys, revealing the source code of the website. Marco copied a few things, opened up a window, and dropped chunks of the site into his code editor.

"What does that even mean?" Grady asked, pretty sure he sounded stupid to Marco.

"Since this site serves all sorts of people around the world who want to generate and decode anagrams, they hit busy times," Marco said. "Sometimes it limits how long the phrase can be. When I built a modified version for myself, I was able to remove that server restriction."

"Since you were the only one using it," Grady said. "Nice."

Marco typed in a few things and studied his screen.

"So, what I'll need to do is download the source of the anagram finder code, but modify it locally," Marco whispered, more to himself than anyone. "I can make a version that only includes names, which should yield us quite different results."

Grady watched for a moment and marveled at how quickly Marco was typing in commands and lines of code Grady didn't understand.

"This might take a while," Marco admitted.

Grady sat back and watched Ava work. She was still tinkering with her small device.

"What are you doing?" Grady asked.

Ava glanced at Grady and then nodded to her desk. "I'm working on a light-sensitive little gadget," she said. "You're going to think it's kind of goofy, though."

"Almost all of this stuff is goofy to me," Grady admitted. "Then again, I had to start over on creating my website like four times last week."

"Okay," Ava said, moving the device closer. "What I'm working on is something that will trigger when the light turns on. So, let's say you like video games."

"I like them, but I definitely don't love them as much as you do," Grady said.

"That's okay," Ava said. "Nobody does. Anyway, what I've done is code into this device a way so that when the light goes on, it will move these little appendages and turn on my game console. For fun, I've added a sound chip."

"Like what?" Grady asked, suddenly fascinated.

"Here," Ava said. "Check it out."

She flipped a switch on the device and covered it with her hands. When she removed her hands from the little device, a small little rod on the machine moved. A small voice that was obviously Ava's chirped from the mini speaker:

"Time for some vids, Ava?"

"Whoa!" Grady shouted. "That's pretty cool!"

Ava smiled.

"I can't take all the credit," Ava said. "Marco let me steal some of his code from his little robot to get the arms to move. This little knob will actually push the button to start up the video games. Kind of like a mini butler."

Grady looked at the little gadget, fascinated. He'd temporarily forgotten all about the dumb pranks he'd been the victim of.

"Can you change what it says?" Grady asked.

"Oh, yeah," Ava replied. "Super easy. I can even change the direction the little arms move by altering the commands."

Marco hit a key on his keyboard and sat back a little.

"Okay," he said. "It's compiling. Now all we have to do is wait . . ."

The bell rang, signaling the end of recess.

"Until coding club," Grady finished.

7

NAME GAME

The three of them went back to their lockers and then to their fifth-period classes. Grady wasn't sure how long it would take for Marco's code to compile, but it didn't matter anyway. He wouldn't know until the end of the school day if his plan even worked.

Grady was thankful that the mysterious April Fools' prankster didn't have any other surprises in store for him. Maybe the final touch was sabotaging his lunch and leaving the longer, more complicated anagram for them to decode.

When the school day ended, Grady practically raced to the computer room. He was disappointed to see that he was the first to arrive.

"Well, this is a first," Mrs. Donovan said. "You're usually the last to come in, Mr. Hopkins."

"Yeah, well, we're onto something big, Mrs. Donovan," Grady said. "We're trying to crack a code to see who's been pranking me today."

"Ah, a victim of the old April Fools' nonsense," Mrs. Donovan replied. "Not my favorite day. I heard your locker got a good dusting."

"Yeah," Grady mumbled, sitting down near Marco's workstation. "That's putting it lightly."

After what seemed like forever, almost all the rest of the Codeheads wandered in. Travis Jacobson, Miles, and Ava, followed by Tara Calhoun, who was texting someone on her way in, as usual.

"Where's Marco?" Grady asked, getting anxious. "He didn't go home, did he?"

Ava sat down. "Calm down. He's on his way."

Five minutes later, Marco rolled into the computer room with a slight smile on his face. His laptop was open and powered on.

"I took a peek after last period," Marco admitted. "I couldn't wait."

"Did it work?" Grady asked. "Do we know who it is?"

"It narrowed down the search," Marco said, moving over to his workstation. "And there are a bunch of names."

Grady waited patiently, while Marco opened up his laptop and showed him the results. There were all sorts of names: Rachel, Brock, Rob, Yasir. As he scrolled down the list, Grady tried to think if he knew anyone with those names.

As he scrolled down, Grady realized there were all sorts of names he hadn't even thought of. It was seeming pretty hopeless when a name appeared that made all the sense in the world.

"Becky," Grady whispered.

"Who is—?" Marco began.

"My sister!" Grady interrupted. "She's the one who did it!"

"We don't know for sure," Ava said. "It could be coincidence that her name popped up, too."

Grady nodded. Ava was right. What he was seeing were thousands of goofy phrases that didn't make sense. They needed to see the whole message to confirm it was her.

"Can we isolate just the phrases with 'Becky' in them?" Grady asked. He looked at the other letters. He began to see other letters in the phrases that might help. The letters that spelled out *April Fools'* were also in there. "Maybe make it only show us the ones with April Fools', too?"

"Sure," Marco said. He entered the three words Grady had requested into his search string. A handful of phrases popped up. One of them was exactly what they were looking for:

APRIL BECKY BRO FOOLS GOT HA HA YOU

"It's scrambled," Marco said.

"Yeah," Ava said. "It put them in alphabetical order for some reason."

Grady nodded. He put APRIL and FOOLS together and moved a few of the other words around.

"Ha ha bro, got you," Grady read from the notepad where he'd scratched it all down. "April Fools', Becky."

"Whoa," Ava said. "Nice. But dang, she got you good, Hopkins."

Grady sat back. It all made sense now. Becky had been part of the whole thing from the start. She'd probably unplugged his alarm clock, making him late for school. And that gave her time to stuff a sock in the toe of his shoe.

He looked at his foot and took his shoe off. Inside was a sticker he hadn't noticed before.

"Liars of lop," he read, pulling Becky's calling card off. He wondered if his alarm clock had something similar on it.

Becky must've packed his lunch, too. While he was still sleeping, she could've easily uploaded a bunch of awful country songs onto his MP3 player, messed with his homework, and everything.

"How did your sister get into your locker?" Marco asked. Grady was wondering the same thing and then realized how easy it would be for her.

"She found the combination," Grady whispered, shaking his head.

Their mom kept all of their school stuff in a file folder at their house, including their orientation letters. There, clearly written next to his locker number, was the combination for the lock. Piece of cake. Because he used a padlock for his gym locker, Becky had to put *Cutesy Horsey* magnets all over the outside.

"Wow," Ava said and whistled. "She must really have it in for you. That's some elaborate plan."

"I didn't know she had it in her," Grady said, shaking his head. It was crazy how much she'd messed with his day.

"And she probably got the sawdust from the wood shop," Marco added, putting some of the other pieces together.

"Makes sense," Grady said. "My mom said she left early. I'm guessing that's what she did. Got into school, scooped up some shavings, and put them in my locker. Knowing I was going to be late, she had plenty of time."

Grady thought about all he'd been through and his stomach growled, still hungry from not eating lunch. His little piano-playing

sister had made a gigantic April fool out
of him.

"So what're you going to do?" Ava asked.

Grady looked at his two fellow Codeheads
and an idea quickly formed in his head.

"I'm going to get her back," Grady said.

8

PAYBACK
BALLYHOO

Once Grady got home, he put his plan into motion. Thankful no one else was home yet, he went into the basement. In the closet, there were boxes of old toys that the Hopkins kids were too old for. He sifted through until he found a giant cardboard carton that had BECKY written in his mom's printing in black marker. He opened it up and saw it nearly filled to capacity with her old dolls.

"Creepy," Grady whispered, sifting through the plastic arms, legs, and heads. He pulled out a larger one that Becky used to play with a lot. Dubbed "My Gal Pal," it was as tall as Becky was when she had gotten it at age four. Becky had named it Molly Dolly, and it was the kind of doll with eyes that opened and closed. Her plastic face was worn, but her permanent smile was just what Grady needed.

Satisfied, he pulled Molly out of the box and headed upstairs.

He went to his room and threw the doll onto his bed. It rolled and ended up sitting straight up, as if watching him. He unzipped his backpack and removed the small device that Ava had been working on in the coding club.

"Don't mess this up, Hopkins," Ava warned him before allowing him to take it. "I worked hard on this thing!"

As he set the gadget down, Grady happened to look over at his alarm clock, the numbers on the front still dark. He lifted the clock up and looked at the bottom of it.

Nothing.

He pulled the cord and, as expected, it was loose. Becky had unplugged it. When he had the plug in this hand, he noticed a sticker wound around the end. No surprise at all, Grady found the words LIARS OF LOP printed on it.

"Hardy-har," Grady said, dropping the cord. He'd have to remember to plug it in. For now, he had some work to do.

He opened the back of the doll's shirt and affixed the device to its upper back.

"This is only going to hurt for a second, Molly," Grady said, kind of creeping himself out.

Using a small razor knife he had for building model spaceships, he made two small incisions in the plastic, one in the base of the doll's plastic neck, and another along the shoulder of its right arm.

He pulled the small, rodlike arms from the device and pressed them into the plastic slits. As the metal balls at the end of the gadget's appendages clicked into place, he smiled.

For once, something was going right!

He turned off the light in his room and, stumbling through the dark, made his way back to his bed. Reaching for the device in the dark, he found the little switch and turned it on. For the final test, he flipped his light switch on and watched his plan come to life.

Literally.

"Yes!" Grady cried. As if on cue, he could hear a car pull into the driveway.

Time to move.

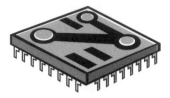

Grady sat crouched in the dark of his sister's room. He'd pulled the shades, turned off the light, and even closed the door. As he sat, waiting, he could hear his mom and Becky downstairs laughing.

Was Mom in on it, too? Grady wondered, but he knew that was ridiculous. His mom would never let him go to school with a can of beets for lunch.

He could hear them talking about dumb stuff, but at one point he heard Becky ask his mom if she thought Grady was home. Holding his breath, he listened, hearing footsteps coming up the stairs. The floor in the hallway creaked.

"Grady?" he heard Becky call. She was probably poking her head into his room, looking for him, he figured. *You're not going to find me in there, sis!*

The footsteps got closer, and he heard them stop outside her door. Peeking around the dresser, he could see the twin shadows of her legs under the gap beneath the door. Her door was never closed unless she was in her room, so it probably made her wonder what was up.

Shoot, Grady thought. *She's not going to open the door!*

Becky opened the door and a second later flipped on the light. Immediately, Grady's creation came to life.

The doll sitting on Becky's bed raised its arm. The head spun around and an eerie voice that Ava was nice enough to record emanated from the doll.

"April Fools', Becky! Come play with me!"

A scream came out of Grady's little sister that he'd never heard before. She stood in the doorway, too frozen to move. He knew then that it was time to gloat.

Grady jumped out and pointed, laughing.

"Got you!" he shouted.

Becky shrieked again, and looked at him as if he were evil incarnate. Becky pointed at the doll, then at him, and then at the doll again, speechless.

"How did . . . ?" she stammered, finally. "What did—?"

"I know," Grady said. "Awesome, right?"

He walked over to the doll and patted it on the back. Grady pointed to the can propped in the doll's lap.

"Did you see the can of beets?"

Becky shook her head, her eyes still wide with fear.

A moment later, their mom came thundering down the hallway.

"What is going on up here?" she demanded. "What happened?"

Neither of them said anything.

"Someone say something!" their mom shouted, looking at the two of them.

"Becky played a bunch of April Fools' jokes on me today," Grady said. "So I played a little one on her. You know, payback."

"He scared the life out of me," Becky gasped, finally able to put coherent words together. "I almost passed out!"

Mom looked at the doll on the bed and at Grady.

"Are those my beets?" she asked, but before either of them could answer, she shook her head. "I don't even want to know."

"So," Grady said, feeling triumphant after a long, rotten day, "we're done with April Fools' Day? No more surprises?"

Becky nodded, catching her breath. "Oh yeah," she said. "We're done."

Their mom sighed. "Get washed up for dinner, you two. I should make those beets just on principle."

"Please don't," Grady pleaded. "I almost had them for lunch."

THE END

1. Grady's day was off to a bad start right from the beginning. What were the clues that things weren't like they usually are? Make a list of clues.

2. No one else seemed to think the things happening to Grady were strange. Were there times when Grady should've realized it was April Fools' Day? Use examples from the book as proof.

3. Grady plotted a quick revenge on his sister for pranking him all day. Do you think he went too far in scaring her? Or are the two even?

WRITE ABOUT IT

1. Grady was the victim of a whole day of April Fools' pranks. Write a story about a time someone played a prank on you. What happened? Did you think it was funny? Be sure to include these details in your story.

2. In this book, the prankster leaves clues in the form of anagrams. Create an anagram out of your first and last name. What is it? Work some of the words from your anagram into a story.

3. Grady wrongly accuses the woodworking class of putting sawdust in his locker. Have you ever blamed someone for something he or she didn't do? Write a story about a time you were wrong and how you made it right.

ABOUT THE AUTHOR

Thomas Kingsley Troupe started writing stories when he was in second grade. Since then, he's authored more than sixty fiction and nonfiction books for kids. Born and raised in "Nordeast" Minneapolis, he now lives in Woodbury, Minnesota. In his spare time, he enjoys spending time with his family, conducting paranormal investigations, and watching movies with the Friends of Cinema. One of his favorite words is *delicious*.

Scott Burroughs graduated from the San Francisco, California, Academy of Art University in 1994 with a BFA in illustration. Upon graduating, he was hired by Sega of America as a conceptual artist and animator. In 1995, he completed the Walt Disney Feature Animation Internship program and was hired as an animator. While at Disney, he was an animator, a mentor for new artists, and a member of the Portfolio Review Board. He worked at the Disney Florida Studio until it closed its doors in 2005. Since 2005, Scott has been illustrating everything from children's books to advertisements and editorials, just to name a few. Scott is also a published author of several children's books. He resides in northern California with his high school sweetheart/wife and two sons.

MORE FUN WITH THE CODING CLUB

GAMER BANDIT

When a mysterious lunch thief leaves behind a card with a website address, Ava Rhodes can't help but check it out. After the site leads her to a really boring online video game, she's even more determined. Can GPS tracking help Ava and her friends find the thief? Or will more lunches go missing?

HACK ATTACK

After a hacker breaches the school's grading system and gives students failing grades, Grady Hopkins wants to set the record straight. Along with coders Ava and Marco, Grady follows a trail of IP addresses as he searches for the perpetrator. Will they find the truth before everyone flunks sixth grade?

ROBOT RESCUE

When his little brother loses the class hamster, Marco Martinez comes to the rescue with a robot and some coding tricks. But will a robot rescue mission be enough to catch this speedy rodent?

READ MORE FROM 12-STORY LIBRARY

Every 12-Story Library book is available in many formats, including Amazon Kindle and Apple iBooks. For more information, visit your device's store or 12StoryLibrary.com.